The Emu Conquest

An Alternate History of the Great Emu War

by

Natasja Rose

Parts of this work appeared as a short story in the Sea Lion Press Anthology "Alternate Australias", under the same pen-name. There is no infringement or duplication committed by publishing this work.

Table of Contents

Acknowledgements

For Lyndal, my editor and my love, whose feedback and laughter during and after the writing process was invaluable.

For the ladies at Pennsic - you know who you are - who inspired this in the first place, and Sea Lion Press, who originally published a short story version in their anthology.

Finally, for Australia's weird and wonderful wildlife, without whose evolutionary horrors I would have had no basis for this story.

Foreword

I acknowledge the traditional owners of Australia, the Aboriginal people, and pay my respects to Elders past, present and emerging.

This book contains references to social, political and racial attitudes and events that were once common, but never acceptable.

The inclusion of these events and attitudes should not be taken as a reflection of the Author's opinions, nor those of anyone else involved in the publication of this book.

Prologue

"The Emu command had evidently ordered guerrilla tactics, and its unwieldy army soon split up into innumerable small units that made use of the military equipment uneconomic."

-Ornithologist Dominic Serventy

Campion, WA, November 8, 1932

The first battle of the Great Emu War...

Major Meredith mused on the fickle nature of notoriety. A week ago, he had been on track to becoming a Colonel, perhaps even a General. Now, he was destined to become a nation-wide joke, at best. His only consolation was that Minister Pearce would share that fate.

It was meant to be an easy mission, a cull of the emu population that saw the newly-cultivated farmland as an easy food source, and destroyed the fences intended to keep out rabbits and foxes. The veteran farmers had laughed when he had led 20 men under two Sergeants, two Lewis machine guns and ten thousand rounds. Overkill, they said, and Meredith had agreed. Machine guns had proven effective in the Great War, killing thousands of the most highly-evolved species on the planet. A bunch of oversized birds would be like shooting fish in a barrel.

Or so they had thought.

It was meant to be an easy mission, an easy victory, that turned out to be anything but.

The birds had been organised. Even to himself, an eye-witness to the horrors the

Emu Army had perpetuated, it sounded absurd. The reality, however, was the furthest thing from laughable.

A runner approached his position at a sprint, caring less for subtlety than for the urgency of his message. "Sir! They have reinforcements!"

The Major paled, "How? We've been fighting every emu this side of the continent for the past week!"

The runner, doubled over and panting for breath, shook his head, "Not emus, sir. They - *down!*"

Major Meredith instinctively hit the ground before the runner could tackle him. Instinct had him rolling into the relative shelter of the base of the nearest machine gun. It probably saved his life.

Lethal, velociraptor-like talons closed inches from his face as the red eyes of a cassowary glared down at him, readying for another kick. The runner screamed as he was lifted into the air by a squad of four wedge-tailed eagles (female, by their size) working in tandem. Around him, similar scenarios were repeated, those who managed to get under shelter pinned down and forced to watch helplessly as their comrades were carried off.

A horrible screeching filled the air, before black feathers and a red beak clouded his vision. The sound of a sickening crack registered just before the blinding pain of a broken limb. Swans. Even the bloody state mascot had turned on them.

Wonderful. Now the Emus had shock troops and an Air Force. Major Meredith could only pray that they didn't come up with a Navy equivalent consisting of Albatross and Penguins, too...

Home Front

Parliament House, September 3rd, 1939, Year 7 of the Great Emu War

Listening to the MPs shout over each other in a haze of white noise, Prime Minister John Curtin wondered if it would be beneath his dignity to pinch the bridge of his nose and yell at them all to shut the hell up.

Probably, he finally decided, but it was still tempting.

After a moment's thought, he pasted on his best approximation of the disappointed expression his mother had aimed at him when he announced his decision to enter politics, and waited. Apparently, no few of the MPs had faced similar expressions from their own mothers, because they quickly fell silent, shamefaced. Apparently, some things did transcend the political divide.

Reasoning that it had worked so far, Prime Minister Curtin attempted his wife's attitude when breaking up squabbles between their children. "Now, take turns and let each other talk. Arguments for and against joining the war."

The leader of the opposition, for once in agreement with Curtin (not that the Prime Minister would ever say so and risk an about-face) stood up. "We've been asking for Commonwealth assistance for three years, since the blasted birds started encroaching on the Sandy Desert. Where was all this 'Commonwealth Unity' then?"

It was a valid point, and one that politicians and public alike had been grumbling over. Curtin nodded to the Deputy Leader of his own party, who looked mildly put out at having his thunder stolen. "As they say in the conscription speeches, 'from each according to his ability'. We are not able to commit all of our forces, not with Japan and Russia looking South and our own ongoing conflict. We are obligated to send some troops, or re-negotiate a lot of treaties, but we can rationally claim that the majority are needed on the Home Front."

That was a good phrase, and one that Curtin could use when he wrote to the King and Churchill. Not that he trusted Churchill to organise a piss-up in a brewery, after that disastrous Greek campaign that had allowed Curtin to unseat Menzies in the first place. Focussing on their own borders was undoubtably the better option, especially the Northern and Western ones.

Offering to let other nations use Australia as a staging ground for Pacific offences might be an option for placating the rest of the world. Perhaps some of the countries currently laughing at Australia might get a sharp look at what they were dealing with, too. Beef up the medical and RAAMC and relief effort divisions, too; he'd been meaning to do that anyway, but now he had a justification that no-one could argue with.

They'd have some battalions ready to mobilise out of Sydney if New Zealand asked, but until then, Australia would wait to be attacked before they retaliated.

* * *

February 19th, 1942, Torres Strait off the coast of Darwin, Year 10 of the Great Emu War

Airman 3rd Class Yamamoto Isamu steadied his nerves, keeping his place in the flight of Japanese bomber planes toward the small town of Darwin, and the military base and shipyard it contained.

There had been rumours filtering through intelligence, largely disregarded as absurd or insipid propaganda intended to scare away potential invasions. It wasn't even very good or believable propaganda, and had quite the opposite effect. High Command viewed it as practically an invitation.

Truly, how weak were the Australian forces, to be losing a conflict against birds?

He smiled, seeing a rapidly-growing shadow on the horizon that had to be the coastline, knowing that they were close to their target. Perhaps this would force Australia into the war, rather than sitting it out as the Americans had. That was why High Command had made this mission a priority; Pearl Harbour had roused one side of the Pacific out of their neutrality; perhaps this would do the same.

Isamu's smile dimmed at the sight of a mass of what appeared to be smoke rising from below.

Had someone released their bombs too early, and accidentally hit a fishing boat of some kind? Had another Axis country got to Darwin first, robbing them of their triumph? His question was answered moments later, when the 'smoke' grew close enough to resolve into individual figures. They were too small and too close together to be Allied aircraft, but what -

A blur of black and brown plumage, with a crest the colour of the setting sun, slammed into his viewscreen and bounced off.

Hastily correcting himself from where he had violently twitched the wheel while jumping in his seat, Isamu had done better than many of his fellow airmen. Off to one side, another bomber had veered sharply and collided with a second 'plane, sending both spiralling toward the ground. It was all right, aircraft often collided with passing birds that couldn't get out of the way fast enough.

Then his windscreen was covered in birds, all screeching and pecking at the glass.

Isamu had only just cleared them off with a sharp jerk when another one landed on the roof of the cabin with a thump and dug its claws into the tiny ledge above the windshield. Upside down, head cocked to the side, Isamu would swear that its piercing golden eye glared into his. There was a determined gleam in the fierce gaze, not unlike the pilots chosen for kamikaze missions.

Isamu had only seconds to regret that comparison, before the bird launched itself forward. At first, he hoped that it was retreating, but clearly the Ancestors were busy watching over someone else. There was a flurry of feathers and a screech that sounded like a death knell, the bird rebounding off the rotor of his front propeller and being sucked into the engine.

If he was to die in a fiery explosion, better to do it closer to the ground, where he and the bombs that his plane still carried might do some actual damage, rather than becoming so much ash and the possibility of a slightly hotter day than the hellscape of this country already was.

Turning his bomber into a steep dive, Isamu winced as several more birds got caught in his propellers, the feathers likely not doing his poor engine any good.

*

Isamu just managed to land the downed plane near a small river, unharnessing himself and scrambling out to a safe distance seconds before it blew up. Perched on a log - one of several he'd used as stepping stones in his dash for safety - the airman could only hope that the explosion had been far enough away not to catch the attention of any military patrols. After a moment, he added the prayer that if it did, that Australian POW camps were more hospitable than the ones back home.

A minute after that, Isamu had cause to regret being so specific in his first wish, when the log next to him opened slit-pupiled eyes and a long jaw with far more teeth than any animal rightfully needed.

Airman 3rd Class Yamamoto Isamu had never been much of a runner - that was why he'd joined the airforce in the first place - but he had surely broken several speed records in his race to get away from the river.

The murky water roiled, churned to foam by thrashing bodies and the sound of rattling hissing growls that quickly became roars not unlike what Isamu though the dinosaurs of ages past might have made.

Many of what he previously assumed to be logs in a particularly cluttered part of the river began moving away from the commotion toward the shore. Isamu decided that being off the river wasn't quite far enough, and bolted up the nearest tree, hoping that the oversized lizards couldn't also climb trees.

He no longer wondered about the war against the wildlife. He just hoped that a military patrol wandered this way soon.

*   *   *

November 27th, 1942, Brisbane, Year 10 of the Great Emu War

US Army Corporal Jack Smithson, the bugger unfortunate enough to be charged with attempting to knock some sense into the rioting hotheads, exchanged tired looks with his Australian counterpart, John Bateman.

Trying to quell a riot was an unusual way to form a sense of camaraderie, but he owed the other man at least a drink after it was all over. Maybe he'd even learn enough slang to understand half of what the bloody Aussies were saying; Sargent Benson kept complaining that he was sure the Australians were filling their reports with incomprehensible slang on purpose. The other Corporal gave a resigned grin, taking a deep breath and opening his mouth to shout some more.

He froze at the cacophony of sharp avian caws, followed by a prolonged warble.

The Australian mob instantly dropped the GIs they were beating up. Many were halfway down the street before Smithson could blink, and those who didn't instantly flee had snapped into defensive positions. He hadn't seen reactions that quick on Parade with the Drill Sargent at full volume! Confused, he looked at Corporal Bateman, who had gone far paler than Smithson thought the situation really deserved. "I'd hoped Intelligence got it wrong. They weren't supposed to have made it so far east..."

East? The Japs were coming from the North, and hadn't risked another incursion after their attempted bombing of Darwin was thwarted by means encoded. Jerry was bogged down in Africa still, relying on their Asian allies to tackle the Pacific arena. "Who? Buddy, you got to give me something to work with here!"

Bateman shook himself. "Brolgas. We didn't think they'd join the Cassowaries after so long competing with each other, but-"

Was now really the time for codewords? Smithson opened his mouth to tell the other man to snap out of it, but his breath rushed from his body as he was tackled. "Everyone, down!"

Then the GIs who weren't unconscious started screaming, and the lights, already at Brownout levels, dimmed further under thousands of winged shapes, silhouetted against the night sky.

Several shapes descended on a GI who was trying to get back to his feet, lifting him several feet into the air before dropping him again. Smithson felt his jaw drop, then an unfamiliar rush of terror as the birds descended again. Beside him, Bateman rolled onto his back and pulled out his sidearm, firing up into the mass of feathers. Around them, the defensive huddles did the same.

A quick glance around showed that he and Bateson were the only officers on the ground, aside from

Sargent Benson, who was currently doing his best to remain *on* the ground. Basic Training had never covered what to do when under attack from the wildlife, so Smithson resorted to the natural fallback of all officers: applying volume to the problem.

*

Later, much later, when they had delegated their least favourite hotheads - army and civilian alike - to cleaning up the carnage, Smithson invited his new friend into the canteen. "So, this shit is why you didn't commit your full forces to the War Effort?"

Bateman looked up from jotting down a report on a napkin, or whatever the Brits and the Aussies called them. "We had our own ongoing War Effort. Wouldn't have done the Allies much good if we'd thrown ourselves into fighting overseas and lost the entire continent."

That was a good point, now that Smithson had experienced the Avian Incursion for himself, rather than a story to be laughed at over drinks. He changed the subject to something less fraught. "So, how are integrated units working out for you lot?"

All right, he probably deserved the Judgemental Stare Bateman aimed at him. Segregated Units were one of the many sore points the Australian and New Zealander crowds had with the Yanks in the first place, and bringing up something that had sparked off the chaos of the last two days in the first place could be considered a little tactless.

Interlude

In Australia, the birds had been united in their goals: getting the humans to stay in their own territory and leave them alone.

For the rest of the Avian world, the goals were a little more nebulous. What the humans called 'civilisation' and non-domestic wildlife called Badlands (Birds didn't have a word for 'apocalyptic hellscape', *yet*…), had been around for longer, had spread further and faster, and would be almost impossible to dislodge without the kind of destruction that rendered the land uninhabitable for everyone. The majority of Asia, Europe and the Americas would not come together quickly as Australia had, lacking the common cause that they did.

But all things come in time, and word was starting to spread...

*   *   *

32nd Street Naval Base, San Diego, California, August 31, 1947, Year 15 of the Great Emu War

Word of the Australian Affair spread slowly but surely across the globe.

Enjoying a quiet walk before some unfortunate ensign came running with the latest crisis, Division Officer Bryant and Division Chief Petty Officer White affected very serious and businesslike expressions, the better to discourage others from interacting. Bryant stepped around a large cluster of bird droppings, and pretended ignorance of the swearing and shaken fists by the poor sap who had just finished cleaning that section of the deck.

Well, the cadet had probably done something to earn the punishment from his sergeant; there was always one who came in convinced of his own superiority. White shot the boy a sidelong look, and went back to feigning his own bout of temporary deafness. "The bird watchers claim that the albatross migratory patterns have been all over the place since the war. Then there's the wild fairy stories the men brought back from Australia."

Bryant spared a moment to ponder whether 'bird watchers' referred to hobbyists or actual scientists, and decided that it probably didn't matter, in the grand scheme of things. "The beer is stronger down there, I'm told, and they were in the middle of a riot. Not hard to get confused in the heat of the moment."

That, or some silly prank aimed to have the reporting party's squad giggling in their bunks while the poor sucker got shouted at. Bryant had dealt with enough of those as an officer, and found the best way to deal with it was to put the lot of them on fatigues until they formed common ground in complaining about him. From the spark in White's eye, he was remembering the same, even as he went back to watching the birds. "True enough, true enough... that's unusual, though, normally albatross and gulls can't get within pecking distance of each other without a fight."

Now that White mentioned it, that was odd. Well, let the brainiacs work it out, now that they weren't scrambling to stay ahead of the Nazi scientists. "Count your blessings. Last time they had a sky scuffle, Captain says it set off one of the air raid alarms. Try explaining *that* to high command!"

White laughed appreciatively, before another albatross emptied it's bowels on the swearing cadet's upturned face. Repressing a few choice words of his own at overly energetic youngsters, Bryant led the way to stop the young idiot from diving over the side to strangle the bird.

White followed, with one last glance skyward. It really was odd behaviour. If birds were cadets, he'd almost compare it to a couple of squads planning mischief...

* * *

Kettle River Valley, British Columbia, March 15, 1954, Year 22 of the Great Emu War

Geese, as any farmer will tell you, have never needed an excuse to make trouble.

This, as Joshua Farmer (and yes, he'd heard all the jokes, thank you for not making more) was finding out, was a problem. Mostly because it meant that 'everyone' knew that geese were trouble, and the spawn of Satan, and newcomers to farming and poultry rarely knew what they were in for. That was a problem, because it meant that everyone tended to laugh him off when he tried to tell them about changing behaviours, and unusually destructive behaviour.

Joshua's family had been farmers since profession-based last names became a thing, hence the Surname. He read the monthly agriculture journals and kept himself inform of the newest discoveries and advances. The point was, Joshua knew about the challenges of feathered livestock, and this was not as normal as they were pretending.

The screech of something trying to cut metal caught his attention, and he hurried over to where the geese were penned, just in time to see two geese, an Emden and a Toulouse (and how had they got all the way got all the way from western Europe and the UK to the opposite side of Canada?) take flight.

Another teeth-clenching sound, and he turned back to the pen, to see his Canada and Domestic geese formed into an unmistakable, if slightly ragged, line. Even as he watched, the one at the head of the line looked him squarely in the eye, never breaking contact as it charged toward the fence separating the goose enclosure from the chicken coop, beak open and head angled. The 'teeth' that lined the edges of its tongue scraped against the metal, and it flapped off toward the back of the queue, allowing the next goose in line to repeat the process.

After a few minutes of teeth-gritting noise, Joshua managed to scrape his jaw off the ground, and went to tend his other animals.

The geese would wear themselves out before they got through the fencing, and Joshua needed a beer before he had to evacuate the chickens (whose ongoing hostilities with the geese also seemed to be escalating) and repair and reinforce the fence between them.

It might be worth a run to the hardware store to stock up on fencing supplies, too, which would add another two or three hours to his day. Not to mention the teacher meeting at his children's school, which he somehow had to schedule in, with Sarah unwell. Today, the geese were just runny icing on the stale cake.

"Bloody feathered devils..."

*   *   *

Amazon Rainforest, April 25th, 1965, Year 33 of the Great Emu War

If the majority of non-Australian birds lacked common causes to unite them, the New World Vultures didn't.

Every year, their habitats and hunting ranges shrank. Every year, they and their young were killed or poached closer and closer to extinction.

No more.

From the Californian condors, to Yellow-headed Vultures of the Amazon, to the Andean condors and Black Vultures, the word spread.

The Yellow-headed Vultures were the first to put the fledgeling alliance to the test, when loggers came. Acres fell as calls for help travelled as swiftly as they could be flown. Bird-watchers throughout the Americas were very confused when migratory patterns abruptly shifted, New World Vultures converging on the Amazon in unprecedented numbers.

The Californian Condors shared territory with an assortment of raptors, and picked up a few tricks. Bulldozers and saw machines tended to have open cabins, windows open for the hope of a breeze in the rainforest humidity. That was a mistake.

Tucking their wings in an imitation of a raptor's killing dive, the Vultures would come through the windows talons-first, wings flapping and blinding. Water containers spilled, frying electronics. Humans screamed and flailed and lost control of their machines as they tried to either escape or fend off their assailants. If all went well, the machines crashed into each other, or fell into ditches, or had the damaging bits collide with large rocks, rendering them temporarily unusable until they were fixed or replaced.

That tactic lasted only as long as it took for the machines to be re-designed, resembling nothing so much as army tanks, made to be as impenetrable as possible. Still, it was not an insurmountable problem. The natives of the Amazon had a less fractious relationship with the birds than the once-colonisers did, and were no happier about the destruction of their home.

Hands wove nets, and moved rocks. Vultures learned to work in teams. Dropped from a great enough height, even a small rock could cave in the roof of a logging machine.

International companies and logging businesses could complain as much as they liked - and did - but if they wanted to stop the Vulture Alliance, or the humans helping them, they would need to get at them, first.

*   *   *

Somewhere in the American Midwest, October 21st, 1978, Year 46 of the Great Emu War

Turkey farmers had been noticing a pattern, of late. Namely, the number of bald eagles, which had been making a slow but steady come-back, very pointedly hanging around the kill-yards of the processing plants when the time came to slaughter the turkeys in anticipation of the Thanksgiving rush.

Normally, there would be a lack of concern when a non-turkey wound up being killed along with America's tastiest mascot, but killing a bald eagle was something that resulted in large fines and prison sentences. As an endangered species, many of them were tagged, tracked, and therefore a lot harder to cover up when they 'accidentally' died. Thus, the slaughter had to be interrupted while the overly-patriotic glorified seagull was intercepted and removed.

More and more frequently, this was taking hours, including some poor schmuck" who had to parkour around the rafters chasing the bloody thing down long enough for someone to get their arms around the wings and take it outside.

By which point, half the turkeys had taken advantage of the distraction and escaped, needing to be either rounded up again, or written off as a loss. Dismally anticipating yet another meeting with the board on behalf of annoyed shareholders, Foreman and Under-Foreman exchanged glances. "Are we sure these feathery pests really need to be on the endangered list?"

The Under-Foreman shrugged. "Could be worse. I've got cousins in Australia, and the stories they tell..."

The Foreman winced in sympathy. Even if the stories coming from Down Under were as much fantasy as fact, a bald eagle was far less trouble than a wedge-tail, or any of the other raptors they had.

Stalemate

Maralinga nuclear testing site, September 29th, 1956, Year 24 of the Great Emu War

It was an honour to be selected for the Nuclear Testing taskforce, but Military Scientist Henry Kingsford found himself dreaming of being back in England.

With temperatures in the mid-twenty degrees Celsius, it wasn't as horribly warm or humid as the potential site at Montecello had been - or, God forbid, where they had flown into Darwin - but just different enough to set his teeth on edge. On top of that, the majority of people on the base preferred coffee, which meant that there was hardly a decent cup of tea to be found, and the locals - relatively speaking, the nearest settlement was a few hundred kilometres away - were entirely too jumpy whenever an emu was spotted. All right, they had a good reason to be wary, the recent Emu-Proof Fence that stretched across the border of Western Australia having been less than effective, but it was so unseemly!

The first tests had gone well, and if they continued to go well, perhaps General HQ might be polite enough to believe a story about the climate being disagreeable.

That hope started to fade when one of the scientists who had been tracking the effects of the fallout on the environment entered, trailed by enough officers to signal an emergency general meeting. Most likely the ones blathering about a sudden boost in the birds' intelligence had finally convinced someone to hear them out. Bother. "What's happened now?"

One of the science lackeys set down a tape player. "Tests are consistent; observational, and lab-based alike: there's been a dramatic increase in intelligence, and in measurable brain activity in the latest scans on the ones we managed to capture."

Of course they had. "Do you have any theories as to what triggered this?"

A few lab technicians exchanged looks. "It roughly matches up with the first tests, sir, and nuclear fallout has been known to trigger strange side effects. Montebello has reported similar occurrences."

Kingsford could see the testing site being abolished as soon as the Australian government found out about this, and his career along with it. "That sounds like something out of a comic book."

The lackey with the tape player shrugged. "Be that as it may, sir, they seem to have developed a more sophisticated form of communication."

From the back of the room, someone scoffed. "Good thing we removed the Maralinga Tjarutja before the tests started. Who knows what would have happened with them? There are recognisable patterns, even if none of our teams have cracked them yet."

There did seem to be some kind of underlying rhythm to the extended bird noises, but discussion was forestalled by a clatter as the maid, an Aboriginal girl fresh from a nearby Mission, dropped her broom.

Ah, yes, they did tend to be excitable about animals in their strange legends, but he'd thought it was the job of the Missionaries to stamp out that nonsense. That was the whole point of removing the half-caste children, according to government policy, after all; to assimilate them into white society. It was considered to be for their own benefit, no matter how much those bleeding-heart 'progressives' shouted about institutionalised cruelty and cultural damage.

Well, it wasn't as though she could contribute anything to the meeting. "Go away, you can clean in here later."

The girl bobbed something approximating a curtsy and vanished, joining several of her fellows out in the yard, all talking excitedly.

An Australian scientist with the rough accent common to rural areas snapped his fingers suddenly. "That's why it's familiar! It sounds like some of the songs the Blacks kids used to sing, before the missionaries trained them to stop jabbering and speak English."

Could intercepting and breaking the code be so very simple? Kingsford brightened a little. "Can we get some translators in here to find out? We should at least test the theory."

The few Australians shared awkward looks. "Not that simple, I'm afraid. The Missions actively work to stamp out the culture and language, and the ones who weren't Mission-raised don't have much reason to help."

That was an understatement. It might be more accurate to say that everyone of Aboriginal descent had a number of reasons to thwart and hinder any translation efforts, whether out of revenge or spite. Fortunately, this particular headache could be placed firmly in the category of 'Not My Problem'.

Kingsford resisted the urge to massage his temples. "Get the Chief Protector of Aborigines on the phone. He can deal with whatever is appropriate to bring to the negotiation table if we want to get on top of this."

*   *   *

Honeysuckle Creek, July 17th 1969, Year 37 of the Great Emu War

Jane Smith, a cleaner at the station of space-related machinery generally known as The Big Spyglass in a case of typical Australian understatement, clustered around the television in the local pub.

Beside her, another woman was giggling, far more enthusiastically than the rather potent cocktail warranted. Jane resisted the urge to swat the girl, and settled for hushing her. She wasn't wrong to be giggling, precisely; most of the pub was hiding grins or attempting to stifle laughter.

Granted, the shouted argument was difficult to hear, with all the transmission static, and extremely one-sided, but what they could hear made for hilarious listening.

It was also a brilliant example of the kind of impending beat-down that drew a crowd.

Jane winced as the static cleared, enough to distinguish a distinctly American accent "...drink a Fosters, you bloody Kiwi!"

Neil whatsit and Buzz whoever had best hope that space-suits hadn't accommodated for the burning desire to punch someone. Jane gave whichever one had spoken credit for an impressive two-for-one insult, and for the spate of swearing as the Honeysuckle Creek telescope tracked a sudden burst of speed from the Australian shuttle, allowing it to pull ahead in the neck-and-neck race to land on the moon. She nudged her giggling co-workers. "The next rocket fuel: spite, outrage, or the universe having a Larrikin sense of humour?"

She'd spoken in a brief lull of noise, and laughter spread around the bar. They all fell silent again at the sound of a triumphant shout, "Beat that, farm-boy!"

The bartender, in a brief respite from pouring drinks, grinned. "Do you think they realise that the entire world is listening to them right now?"

Jane sniggered, wondering if her paycheque would cover another drink. Probably not, she reluctantly concluded; domestic work was chronically under-paid, when it was paid at all. "Still, mankind on the moon! Whatever next?"

A young soldier, probably an unfortunate victim of the recent Conscription trial, scowled over a VB. "An Earth-like planet with less hostile wildlife? Maybe we can migrate there and get away from the bloody birds!"

The moon landing was temporarily forgotten as the entire pub toasted that notion.

* * *

Queen Victoria Park, Sydney, August 19, 2006, Year 74 of the Great Emu War

What would later be known as the Urban Warfare of the Great Avian Conquest started off fairly innocuously.

Michaela Rios had been celebrating the newest milestone in her physical therapy with a trip to the park, her carer keeping a wary eye on the sky while Michaela awkwardly fed the last of their lunch to the pigeons.

That was safe; the pigeons had agreed to a neutral stance in the Avian War. It wasn't ideal, by any stretch of the imagination, and it earned the birds no favours from either side. Still, it was nice to have at least one thing with wings that didn't want to kill you.

Well, it *was* safe, until a tell-tale squawk came down from the sky.

Michaela's carer turned as white as the logo on her blue uniform shirt. The soldiers patrolling around the park all instinctively dove flat on the ground. Michaela wished she'd gotten just a little further in her physical therapy; a mechanical wheelchair might not be fast, but it was better than being stranded if anything happened to her carer before they escaped.

The magpies, with an unfortunate amount of self-preservation, bypassed the people with guns and went straight for the more vulnerable targets.

Michaela had never known her carer use that kind of language before. Or to have such good aim, as she hurled the last of the sandwiches at the rapidly-descending tiding of magpies. At the same time, she swept the folded blanket off Michaela's legs, throwing it over both of their heads as she huddled protectively over the wheelchair.

Michaela braced herself, blind to the danger outside the blanket but all too aware of the flurry of hundreds of wings all beating at once and the thunderous squawking. When the expected clawing failed to occur - and there were no cries of pain suggesting that it was happening to someone else - she cautiously lifted a corner of the makeshift shelter to peer out.

There was a furious battle going on, but *not* between the expected parties.

Rather than half-blinded humans trying to fend off a magpie attack, the pigeons had launched a co-ordinated offensive against the magpies, apparently over the discarded sandwiches, currently impaled on magpie claws.

Cautiously lowering the blanket and rubbing a bruise from one of the wheelchair handles, Michaela's carer pulled out her work phone to record video footage, while a soldier radioed for back-up. "I don't even want to think about the kind of paperwork this Incident Report is going to cause."

Another soldier, gun still at the ready in case either side of the avian air fight remembered that there were non-flight-capable targets around, nudged her foot sympathetically with his own. "The first break-through in decades, and it was a civilian who isn't even vaguely associated with the military. Our Sargent is going to have *words*. Loud, sarcastic ones."

Michaela's carer nudged back. "Maybe the government will actually start funding us like we're worth."

They exchanged glances, and burst out laughing. "Yeah, I know. Chance would be a fine thing. At least formalising whatever comes out of this is someone else's problem."

The soldier tried to look serious as a uniformed officer glanced over at them.

"Might I interest you in dinner while we try to avoid the notice of our superiors?"

The carer carefully ignored Michaela's cackling as she smiled. "That sounds lovely."

The Beginning…

August 26, 2019, Parliament House, Canberra, ACT, Year 87 of the Great Emu War

Being a political aide was a thankless task.

Being a political aide deemed expendable enough to deliver bad news to the Prime Minister was even worse. Luckily, Fatima was a Millennial; thankless jobs and being a convenient scapegoat came with the age bracket.

She kept well away from the theoretically-bird-proof windows, wondering for the millionth time why the Government insisted on keeping the full-length frames. Scanning her pass, she entered the office.

"Bad news, sir. Scouts say that we've lost Ivanhoe and Wilandra."

They were far western towns, not quite on the border, but still a good eleven or twelve hours by car. A man with the stars of a General looked grim. "Then we must assume that South Australia has fallen or surrendered. Most of the Territory has been in league with the bloody birds for a decade or so; we can't count on support from them."

A politician who was somehow still on the frontbench, despite coming up with racist statements to blurt out during Q&A every other week that would have seen anyone else fired with prejudice, rolled his eyes. "You say that like it's surprising. Every time we try to build on this ceremonial field or that sacred tree, the Intelligence translators go on strike, and we lose even more territory and infrastructure!"

A backbencher, the one member of the party with Indigenous heritage, gave the speaker a flat look. "Oh, no. I can't imagine how horrible that might be."

Fatima would have scored that as a five-point hit, but the ruling party tended to be oblivious to such pointed sarcasm. That made Fatima's next bit of news even worse. "The latest reports claim that the feral goats in the rural areas were holding the line, but the Wedge-Tails started to weigh in a few days ago, and it's turned to a fighting retreat." She checked her notes, "We haven't heard from Tenterfield or Kyogle in over a week, either, not since Queensland stopped responding. Byron Bay says they're holding out, but besieged on all sides."

Byron Bay had stopped being a tourist paradise back in the early 70s, along with most other coastal towns, when a Maritime Avian assault resulted in a massacre of beachgoers. The attack having come in the wake of a large oil spills near Newcastle, Australian Environmental laws swiftly got a lot tougher, and the fines very nearly paid for the new army/naval bases that sprung up as a result.

Another General scowled, "Albury-Wodonga report similar sieges. They're closing in on us. The pigeons and seagulls are still on our side and protecting the cities proper, but they won't move out of suburban and city areas, and their demands are increasing."

Of course they were. Both species bred at ridiculous rates, which was great for keeping up numbers in the Urban Avian Defence Force. Unfortunately, it also meant greater competition for food, which meant more relying on humans for feeding. If they lost the agricultural areas, even that might be at risk.

The Prime Minister noticed that Fatima had yet to depart, despite the glares being aimed in her direction by One Nation.

How they remained in power at all was honestly baffling. How bad did home have to be for someone to attempt coming to a land that was losing a war against the wildlife? Immigration by the desperate - and other countries imposing environmental refugee travel restrictions - was the only reason Australia maintained the much-reduced population size it had.

The "Prime Minister of Marketing", as many of the younger generations called him, gestured impatiently. "Unless you have more news to tell us, I'm sure you've got better places to be."

Fatima bit back the first several responses that came to mind, most of which would get her fired with prejudice, trying to maintain a calm expression. She'd been hoping that some other poor sap could be stuck presenting the news that was already raging like last month's bushfires - bad enough to cause a temporary cease-fire in conflict zones across the continent - through the Parliamentary Break Rooms. "It seems that the... ah, the situation has spread, sir."

For a moment, Fatima almost thought she was about to see the leader of a nation abandon dignity enough to bang his head on the table. Not that dignity had been in high supply, with the last three Prime Ministers. Unfortunately, the Senior Politician colloquially known as Mr Potato Head everywhere that he wasn't within earshot intervened before the PM had to make that choice. "How so?"

Fatima was spared from attempting to explain details she didn't have by another General, who had apparently just received the memo. "Central and South America have been battling New World Vultures since the 60s, but there are reports going back as far as the end of the Second World War. The last allied troop manoeuvres, where we pulled in help from the United States and Old Mum... well, reports are that some sea-birds might have made it back home with them and spread the word, and now the birds have finally pulled themselves together enough to organise their own Resistance."

The Prime Minister's expression cleared, before dropping abruptly. "Oh, that must be what the Posh Bugger and the Grand High Tangerine were banging on about over the phone yesterday! I don't remember either of those countries having much to worry about by way of birds."

The Opposition Leader, the latest in a string of fairly unremarkable older white men, offered a half-shrug. "Probably more upset about it happening at all. We've had jokes about the wildlife trying to kill us since the continent was discovered, but people will laugh a lot harder at America and the UK, if they end up in the same predicament."

The Prime Minister glared across the central table - a comfortable return to normality in the midst of chaos. "He was blathering on about turkeys gone mad! It was all I could do not to tell him that he had to narrow it down if he wanted me to know which member of his inner circle he was talking about!"

Fatima couldn't wait to share that during the next smoke break. Bagging out Leaders who richly deserved it didn't count as exposing political secrets when every other country in the world was doing the same thing. (Adekunbo, from the Moroccan Embassy, had some beautiful nicknames, few of which translated into English) "An easy mistake to make, Mr Prime Minister."

The Prime Minister glared across the table at the Leader of the Opposition, who leaned back in his chair with the relaxed smugness that had been aimed at the Opposition for so many years, the last time they were in power. It was the calm assurance of a man facing a crisis and knowing that he won't be taking the fall for it. The Prime Minister lost the battle of wills and returned to his rant, "The bald eagle is a glorified seagull, and they don't have anything on the emu scale. I don't know what they're complaining about."

The first General from earlier glanced up from his tablet, where he'd either received a far more detailed memo, or taken advantage of the dick-measuring contest to do a quick Google search. "The USA has the turkey and trumpeter swan, ranked at 8 and 14 in terms of size, and their bald eagle. Numerous but not very aggressive, I imagine turkey dinners are about to become either very rare, or a lot more popular."

Someone from the Independent section sniggered, but on the whole they were somewhat better at not acting like a session of Parliament was a high school Drama Club. The General regally ignored the interruption. "The UK has a few varieties of eagle, but on the small side, and not many of them. Their biggest problem is likely to be the geese."

The Leader of the Opposition in the Senate, third in command of the Labour party and proof that some people cared more about whether you could do the job than what colour your skin was, raised a sarcastic eyebrow. "Literally or figuratively?"

One of the Tasmanian Independents, who usually swung wildly between badly expressing a valid point and spouting a controversial opinion only loosely based in fact, took the question at face value. "Both,

I expect. Vicious buggers, and far too numerous for anyone's taste even when they weren't in active rebellion."

It would have been interesting to stick around for the debate on how to deal with the matter, but someone needed to kick the latest Nepotism Hire out of the break room and remind him that he still had actual work to do, and Fatima had a lot more messages to run. One of which was to hint to the catering staff that tempers were likely to be short, and to expect at least one Member to take their bad mood out on the tea lady.

Doubtless she'd hear about it in Question Time or on social media before the day was out, anyway.

...Of The End

The humans were losing.

If Warrant Officer 1st Class Pryce was honest with himself, they had been losing since the first skirmish with the wretched birds. He glanced at the Australian Coat of Arms proudly blazoned on his shoulder; the imposing kangaroo across from the vaguely absurd and decidedly not-to-scale platypus.

It had been an emu across from the 'roo, once, according to the history books, before a referendum was held in 1935, two years after the emus declared war, to choose a replacement. In the true Larrikin spirit, Australians had voted en masse for the most ridiculous possibility. In his quiet moments, Warrant Officer Pryce liked to imagine the frustrated swearing that must have echoed through Government House when the results came through.

Regardless, someone up on Capitol Hill had decided that it would serve them right to be stuck with Nature's idea of a practical joke on every official backdrop and government letterhead for the rest of time (or until the bigwigs got around to doing something about it), and there they were.

A tell-tale caw offered a split-second of warning. Two centuries of evolutionary survival instinct kicked in, and Officer Pryce ducked. There was a distinctive rasping sound as claws raked across his helmet, and the magpie shot him a malevolent stare as it spiralled up for another round.

Officer Pryce did his best to keep the bird in his peripheral vision as he scanned the sky for more of the flying demons. Reports had that they'd started travelling in flocks recently, and it was better to determine whether there was cause for concern before he raised the alarm. No-one wanted to go on lockdown and cause a nationwide panic for a single magpie.

Legend had it that, once upon a time, the winged menaces had only attacked if they thought their nests were threatened. That one, Officer Pryce wasn't sure he believed; the wretched things took far too much pleasure in dive-bombing everything that moved. It had reached the point that no-one didn't know several people who had lost at least one eye to a magpie assault, and partial blindness no longer qualified for a Disability pension.

His sister claimed that it was a step forward for Accessibility in the Public Forum, and for Disability rights in general. Officer Pryce thought that the Government had taken a look at the numbers and decided to save themselves a few million a year.

His scanning pattern reached the tree line, and his heart skipped a beat. A black mass hovered at the horizon, and the underbrush rustled in a way that no amount of wind could explain. He fumbled for his whistle, blowing as hard as he could.

At the other guard-points, the same shrill noise echoed, over and over. A stampede of pounding feet indicated the arrival of backup, and he dropped the whistle in favour of his rifle. Two privates scrambled into flanking position beside and slightly behind him, one taking over whistle duty and the other sliding into a firing stance. The birds weren't in range yet, but it wouldn't be long.

Fatima hadn't heard this much screaming in Parliament House since the last time the

Greens tried to introduce a bill reducing Parliamentary Pensions to something more in line with what the average Australian received, and only applicable to ex-politicians of actual retirement age.

Outside, the thrum of thousands of wings mingled with the cacophony that was human voices shouting and a dozen different species of birds shrieking back, the rat-tat-tat of rapid gun-fire just barely audible over the rest of the noise. She sprinted down a hallway with a gaggle of other Aides and Administrative Staff, tucking a stray lock of hair back under her headscarf. Wearing her actual hijab generally wasn't worth being interrogated every time she got within shouting distance of One Nation, but if this was to be her last day on earth, Fatima wished she had worn it, and told anyone who objected to go choke.

There was another loud thump as another magpie dove at the windows, claws first. That had been going on at every window in the building, each bird hitting the same spot. The glass stood up to bullets, but even the most defensive measures could only take so much.

A crack appeared in the glass; no bigger than a twig, but a fatal weakness. Another dive, and the crack spread in a lightning pattern, Nature's fury in feathered form. A cawing chorus of triumph rose above the din, and the humans ran faster.

The safe-room was only a few minutes away. Surely they wouldn't close it until Parliament House was actually breached.

Hopefully the non-combatants inside had heard the alert over the collective tantrum that passed as most sessions of Parliament these days; they couldn't spare anyone to run in and tell them personally.

Fatima didn't swear, as a general rule. To react to such insults was to give in to ill-will. Right now, 'ill-will' was the very least of what she was feeling.

They had arrived at the safe-room to find half of Parliament - the Opposition, Greens and Independent half - gathered outside the closed door to the safe-room, a few muffled but very familiar voices shouting from within that they'd open the door when the birds were gone.

One of the Greens Senators, usually noted for her composure, was pounding on the door and swearing up a storm. Fatima didn't blame her, and might have joined in, if helpless rage hadn't rendered her breathless and speechless.

The gunfire had almost stopped, and for a moment she thought they might be safe. Then the sound of shattering glass echoed through the halls like a bell tolling the death-knell, and the cries of birds grew closer. A One Nation aide reached for Fatima's hand, political and humanitarian differences forgotten in the face of impending death. She squeezed it gently, offering a prayer to Allah and the Prophet.

Not for her life - she wasn't sure even they could grant that - but for at least a painless death.

A few soldiers staggered through the door, slamming it behind them. They were bleeding heavily from a slash wounds, but still tried to drag some of the furniture over as a barricade. One of them, a Warrant Officer if Fatima remembered her ranking symbols correctly, glanced around in confusion. "What are you all doing still out here?"

The Leader of the Opposition in the Senate gestured in wordless frustration at the locked door, and Fatima clarified. "Brings a new meaning to pulling the ladder up behind you, doesn't it?"

The Warrant Officer didn't share Fatima's aversion to curse words, and indulged fit to turn the air blue. In a slightly more level frame of mind, he glanced around. "Right, our options are limited. We don't know how the entire Avian Armed Forces got so close so fast, but they have, and they're not leaving. We can surrender and hope for mercy, or we can keep fighting and repeat the Massacre of Ma Ma Creek."

Fatima winced; photos of the small town outside of Brisbane, wiped off the map last year along with its 150-odd residents, had haunted her nightmares for weeks.

Last month's Nepotism Hire, who Fatima remembered mostly for his tendency to pin the blame for his failures on anyone and everyone else spoke up, a totally unreasonable note of indignant outrage colouring his protest. "And what about the ones who fought and died for us?"

The Warrant Officer's expression clearly questioned what the hell a youth whose biggest claim to fame was who his parents were might know about personal sacrifice. "They're dead; they don't get a say."

One of the newer Premiers piped up, aiming a glare at the locked door of the safe-room, "Face it, we've been in a fighting retreat for decades. We lost all of Western Australia within a year, and all attempts at an emu-proof fence to match the rabbit-proof one have been temporary at best, and abject failures at worst!"

She wasn't wrong, and Fatima cast a speculative look at the proof that their leaders didn't care about anyone except themselves. "Do you think the emus would accept the symbolic sacrifice of offering up our leaders?"

The voices from inside the safe-room faltered, before the shouting resumed at a very increased volume. Most of the room ignored them. The Warrant Officer shrugged. "No idea, but if you can look me in the eye and claim that you believe that we'll be worse off under the birds than we are now under those gutless cowards, then I'll concede the point and die on my feet."

A few of the Ruling Party's aides, abandoned to luck and Fate, tried. They really did. Fatima sympathised, to an extent. Humans should be governed by humans, not by birds who still remembered being dinosaurs.

But in the end, they couldn't.

Fatima sighed. "Well, I for one, welcome our new Avian Overlords. Now, how do we get the message across to birds who don't speak English."

The Officer grimaced. "They've developed a very primitive writing system. I'll translate."

Epilogue

One year Post-Surrender...

The semi-peaceful transition of power had gone smoothly, and an uneasy sort of co-operation had resulted once the emus and their army admitted that some things were a lot easier with opposable thumbs.

The mass re-working of the Social Contract and the Political System had been... complicated, to say the least, but eased by the fact that other parts of the world were also battling their own natural inhabitants who decided that they couldn't muck things up any worse than the humans had. Native minorities were enjoying unprecedented power in the conquered territories, most of them having a long history of working with Nature, rather than attempting to subjugate it. There was a bitter irony in that somewhere, but not one that anyone cared to examine too closely.

Perhaps the Australian Conflict would re-start, one day, with the same or different results. But for now, there was peace.

About the Author

Natasja has been writing since a very young age, though those notebooks have been lost in the Old Schoolbooks Cupboard and (hopefully) will never see the light of day.

Most of her stories, published or otherwise, began life as conversations with friends that sparked an idea that grew into a story or poem.

Her publishing adventures started with poems and short stories in focus newsletters like ABA and AMBA, and online sites like Readwave, NaNoWriMo and FictionPress, before finally taking a chance with self-publishing.

Natasja Rose lives and works in Sydney, Australia, but travels whenever she can.

Her greatest wish is to visit all the places in the world that inspired her writing as a child and create new stories for new inspirations

By the Same Author

THE HIGHWAYMAN'S LEGACY

Being a Psychic sucks.

It would probably be worse if Tina Barnes had to listen to every random thought that crossed people's mind, but witnessing the death of every person who died in a spectacularly gory fashion is no picnic, either. Being on a tour of Historically Significant (read: haunted) locations isn't really helping.

Oh, and did she mention the supernatural soap opera of two ghosts possessing random people in their bid for a Happily Ever After that usually ends with the hosts dying?

Because that's happening, too.

In a chilling tale of ghostly romance, friendship and fed-up psychics, what was meant to be a normal holiday tour takes a potentially deadly turn into a race against time.

Book One of Ghostly Travels

Available in Kindle ebook and Paperback

Eternity's Invitation

Dealing with her best friend being possessed by the ghost of a star-crossed lover was just the beginning.

Returning to a place where she swore she would never set foot again, Tina Barnes is once again dragged kicking and screaming into the realm of the Supernatural.

At least she has company this time.

In the gripping sequel to 'The Highwayman's Legacy', re-join the usual suspects in a series of ghostly murders that have nothing to do with star-crossed lovers....

And everything to do with destroying anyone who has the potential to stop them.

Book Two of Ghostly Travels

Available in Kindle ebook and Paperback

All You Can Be

Living With Aspergers, by Aspies and those who love them

Asperger's Syndrome affects different people in different ways, from Aspies themselves, to people who have friends or family with the condition.

This is a collection of stories and anecdotes, ranging from the good things about being Aspie, to common coping strategies, to media misrepresentation and how it affects people of all ages and backgrounds.

Being Aspie is far from being all fun and games, but there are definitely far worse things to be.

Book One of Living Diversity

Available in Kindle ebook and Paperback

All That I Need

Childfree by Choice

Raising a family is not for everyone.

Whether because of your incompatible lifestyle, personal reasons or general disinterest in small humans, a growing number of people are choosing not to reproduce. This choice is often perceived as incomprehensible to the general, child-having, populace.

Contained within the book are a series of anecdotes from people who have chosen, for one reason or another, not to become parents. Hopefully, it will increase understanding in the community that just because you don't agree with a choice, doesn't make it wrong or invalid.

Book Three of Living Diversity
Available in Kindle ebook and Paperback

The Temporarily-Misplaced

Collection

More Short Stories, interspaced here and there with the occasional monologue and poem, that didn't quite make it into novels of their own.

Some of them might at a later date, but for now, you can read them here.

Read about the Adventures of Codename Granny, the origins of mermaids, space exploration that doesn't quite go as planned, and reincarnated soulmates that don't always end in Happily Ever After.

A sequel, of sorts, to 'The Lost Collection'.

Book Two of the Anthology Series

Available in Kindle Ebook and Paperback

The Writing Prompt Collection

Short stories, plus the occasional monologue and poem, inspired by writing prompts.

Read about the night-time protectors, a different take on the gingerbread witch, which industry the Millennial Generation is killing this time, and how to REALLY say it with flowers.

A fun read that will have you laughing, crying and groaning by turns, The Writing Prompt Collection is the latest in a series of Anthologies by Natasja Rose.

Book Three of the Anthology Series

Available in Kindle Ebook and Paperback

The Deliberate Collection

Short stories and the occasional poem. Read about Surviving Zombies, Alien Invasions and Dragons. Discover the fate of Jack the Ripper, and how to really get the attention of a vengeful spirit.

Alternating between funny, serious and scary, this collection of written work will keep you engaged until the end

Book Four of the Anthology Series
Available in Kindle Ebook and Paperback

Cinderella Grows A Spine

Cinderella didn't know exactly what prompted her to break free of the cycle of abuse from her step-mother, but one thing was certain: nothing is ever accomplished by waiting for someone else to magically fix things.

After all, Cinderella was a pretty, educated young lady of high birth and good breeding, and her Step-mother didn't control the world, no matter what the woman thought.

It wasn't like she didn't have options...

In a delightful reinvention of the classic fairytale, Cinderella takes charge of her own destiny, and through the power of friendship, courage and liberal applications of common sense, finds her own Happily Ever After

Book One of Timeless Tales, Modern Morals
Available in Kindle ebook and Paperback

Snow White Learns Stranger Danger

People in Fairytales are far too trusting. But what if they weren't?

Snow White learned at a young age that not everyone has good intentions, and that being a Princess didn't mean that everyone loved her.

There were people who were kind without expecting anything in return, and there probably were old beggar-women who were happy to repay a good deed, but this one was far too insistent about being allowed into the house.

In a unique re-imagining of the Classic Fairytale, Snow White learns the value of friendship, sensible precautions, and a good cast-iron skillet.

Sequel to 'Cinderella Grows a Spine'.

Book One of Timeless Tales, Modern Morals
Available in Kindle ebook and Paperback

Red Riding Hood and the Stalker

Appearances can be deceiving, but a person's true nature is impossible to fully hide.

Ruby was getting very, very sick of having to hide out at her grandmothers because it was the only place Adrian Wolfe wouldn't follow her. Really, hadn't anyone ever told him that Stalking was not romantic, and that no means no?

A retelling of 'Little Red Riding Hood', in which Stalking because you "can't stay away" is a giant red flag, and the Big Bad Wolf isn't quite so obviously a Villain. Sequel to 'Snow White Learns Stranger Danger'.

Book Three of Timeless Tales, Modern Morals

Available in Kindle ebook and Paperback

Beautiful, Inside and Out

What do you do when your arrogance and pride leaves you alone in the world? Some people lash out, falling deeper and deeper into darkness. Others learn from the experience, and become better for it. Isabella had never realised how much she would regret driving Sophia away, but she knew that before she could change things between them, she would need to change herself.

In a journey of self-discovery, friendship and the occasional scandal, Isabella realises that true beauty is found within, and that loving someone else is no help if you can't love yourself as well.

A 'twisted fairytale' retelling of Beauty and the Beast. Side-story to "Cinderella Grows a Spine" and "Snow White Learns Stranger Danger".

Book Four of Timeless Tales, Modern Morals
Available in Kindle ebook and Paperback

BETWEEN DARKNESS AND LIGHT

It wasn't Jason's fault that his father's Ultimate Sacrifice hadn't resulted in Martyrdom, but in a Villainous reputation.

It wasn't Evanna's fault that she had been in the wrong place at the wrong time, and would up with Superpowers a la toxic waste.

It wasn't Stretch's fault that his teachers focused more on using his powers than on the ethics of doing so.

In a world where Superpowers are common, and those gifted with them a facet of everyday life, the lines between Hero and Villain are not always so easily drawn.

As though being a teenager wasn't hard enough!

Book One of "Two Sides of the Same Coin"
Available in Paperback and Kindle ebook

TO LIGHT THE WAY IN DARKNESS

The first year at the Superhero Academy ended with a lot of changes, but that doesn't mean that the Super-student's problems are over.

Discrimination is still rife in the ranks, and just because things are changing doesn't mean that the underlying problems have gone away. On top of that, there are several of the 'Old Crowd' who are angry at the reluctant Superheroes as the source of all these changes, and want nothing more than to paint them as Villains.

The younger generation will need to step up their game, and keep a constant watch, if they want to survive to graduate.

Book Two of "Two Sides of the Same Coin"
Available in Paperback and Kindle ebook

A CANDLE IN THE NIGHT

A collection of short stories based around the world and characters from the *"Two Sides of the Same Coin"* trilogy.

Read about Alien Invasions begun and ended in ways that will give future historians some very interesting days at the office, how Supervillains formed their on Council, and how DIY costumes aren't always the best idea.

From Villainous backstories, to relationships, these stories will entertain you in the best of ways.

Side Stories from the "Two Sides of the Same Coin" Trilogy

Available in Paperback and Kindle ebook

The Time Traveller's Seamstress

Time Travel is easy. Fitting in while surfing the time-space continuum is harder.

A big part of the Time Agency's success was due to their costuming department, a variety of men and women who made fantastic clothing... and who really wished that the Agents would pay more attention to details like what year and geographical region they were heading to, and the policy on advanced notice for anything pre-1920s. Honestly, do they think all of that hand-stitched embroider and beading is easy?

A humorous read likely to make you a lot more sympathetic to the costuming department, "The Time-Traveller's Seamstress" is an entertaining book that will keep readers engaged to the end.

Book One of Supporting the Time-Space Continuum

Available in Paperback and Kindle ebook

The Time Traveller's Accountant

The Costuming Department probably had it worse, but life wasn't all roses in Finance, either.

Whether it was sourcing ancient coins in a usable condition, only for the Agents to lose then less than a week later, or trying to convince Management to approve a payroll system from the current century (seriously, did anyone still use paycheques for wages?), it was one problem after another.

You'd think that the other departments would be more sympathetic, given what the agents subjected them to, but no...

An entertaining sequel to the Time Traveller's Seamstress, this book is a fast-paced read that will keep you going until the end.

**Book Two of Supporting the Time-Space
Continuum
Available in Paperback and Kindle ebook**

The Time Traveller's IT

IT is not a glamorous job. Not even when you're troubleshooting time machines.

Between routine maintenance, fixing what the Agents managed to break this week, backing up the mission logs and thwarting attempts to poach their human blockade of a receptionist, the IT Department of the Time Agency rarely has a dull moment.

Honestly, they might spend less time wishing for a meteor strike if they did…

An entertaining new instalment to the Time Traveller's Series, this book is a fast-paced read that will keep you going until the end.

Book Three of Supporting the Time-Space Continuum
Available in Paperback and Kindle ebook

Captive Hearts

No one was entirely sure what had started the conflict with the Grey Mountains, only that there was no end in sight.

When Danae, one of the Vale's most powerful Healers, is taken prisoner in a raid, she finds an unexpected protector: Torrin, the Mountain King's nephew. In fear for her life, Danae is determined to hate the man responsible for her capture, but his kindness and compassion make it increasingly difficult.

Torrin hadn't expected to find himself in charge of a prisoner, especially such a difficult one. He hadn't expected to find her defiance so attractive either. If only she wasn't his prisoner...

Available in Kindle Ebook and Paperback

The Queen's Blade

Sayfiya was raised an assassin, but only the men of her clan are permitted to take contracts. Desperate to prove herself worthy, she plans to kill the queen who has evaded several attempts on her life, planning to succeed where her kinsmen had failed.

Instead, Queen Alexandra offers her a new life, ripe with opportunity. Accepting the offer is a risk, one that may cost Sayfiya more than she ever suspected.

Or it may lead her to something greater than she could have dreamed…

Available in Kindle Ebook and Paperback

THE WAY OF THE EXILED

Owain was a boy when he witnessed the massacre of his family and the loss of his home.

Fleeing into exile with his infant brother and a scattered handful of survivours, Owain must somehow keep them safe and alive as he grows from a traumatised child to a man able and prepared to reclaim his home.

In a tale of loss, hope and the bonds of friendship, family and destiny are what you make of them

Book One of the Exiled Trilogy

Available in Kindle Ebook and Paperback

The Murder Mystery

Ramona Bates thought that a dating site that matched people based on their internet search history was the perfect way to get everyone off her back about her lack of a love-life. Ramona was a crime fiction writer, who was going to have a google history to match that?

When she met Joshua Ryan, a butcher's assistant who knew a surprising amount about murder, it seemed like destiny.

When Ramona released her first book, the local police force realised that a lot of the murder scenes matched with old crime reports. Now they are on the hunt, but will they catch the right person?

In a twisting tale that puts a new spin on both crime and romance, this book will have you holding your breath to the end.

Available in Kindle Ebook and Paperback

Surviving a Zombie Apocalypse

No-one ever thought that the Zombie Apocalyse would actually happen.

If the average person thought about a potential Zombie Invasion at all, it was to mock unrealistic movies or discuss how/if they would survive it. That turned out to be a good thing.

When the emergency call went out that the pandemic that turned its victims into something very like Zombies was not, in fact, a viral hoax, but the real thing, they had a plan.

As it turned out, the biggest danger wasn't the Zombies, but surviving the morons who though they were living a video game and had just figured out that Loot Drops didn't exist in real life…

Available in Kindle Ebook and Paperback

The Protector

All children know about the monsters. The ones under the bed, in the closet, hiding beneath the stairs... All just waiting to jump out and attack.

Children do not know of their protectors, the ones who fight the monsters, who keep the children safe, until they are no longer needed. Sometimes, that lasts a lot longer than physical childhood.

In a tale that combines that fantasy and nostalgia of childhood with the more mature outlook of adult life, The Protector is a book that will leave you longing for more.

Available now in Kindle Ebook and Paperback

Earth: The Fatal Frontier

Earth Technology was no match for the might of the Federation's Advance Research Corps.

Humans - those who survived, at least - preferred the term 'Invading Space Army', amid protests about being experimented upon. The Alien scientists found their quibbling about the ethics of non-consenting test subjects tedious, but admitted that the natives were best suited to help the research teams navigate this Deathworld.

Vera was absolutely holding a grudge over the massacre of the facility where she worked, she knew how to hide emotion and fake compliance. She wasn't a wildlife expert, but the Australian sense of humour bred a wealth of knowledge on how to inflict wildlife on unsuspecting foreigners...

The real battle for Earth's liberation wouldn't be fought between armies, but by a scattered handful of survivours fuelled by spite and a basic knowledge of how to survive a world where everything is designed to kill you.

Available now in Kindle Ebook and Paperback

Whitechapel Justice

Jack the Ripper terrorised the streets of Whitechapel, until the killings stopped as suddenly as they started.

Police were baffled; had the Ripper left the area, or been scared off? Who was he and how had he stayed ahead of the law? Why had he targeted the women? The cases remained unsolved, and History would never know more than rumour and suspicion.

Only a select few would ever know the truth. The streets of Whitechapel take care of their own…

Available now in Kindle Ebook and Paperback

THE EMU CONQUEST